To our sweetheart Verity.
Easter 2000.
With lots of love from:-
Grandma & Grand-dad.
D0299589
THIS WALKER BOOK BELONGS TO:

For Raymond,
brightest and best

First published 1994 by
Walker Books Ltd, 87 Vauxhall Walk
London SE11 5HJ

This edition published 1997

4 6 8 10 9 7 5 3

This book has been typeset in Garamond.

Printed in Hong Kong

British Library Cataloguing in Publication Data
A catalogue record for this book is
available from the British Library.

ISBN 0-7445-5224-9

HUMPHREY THUD

Camilla Ashforth

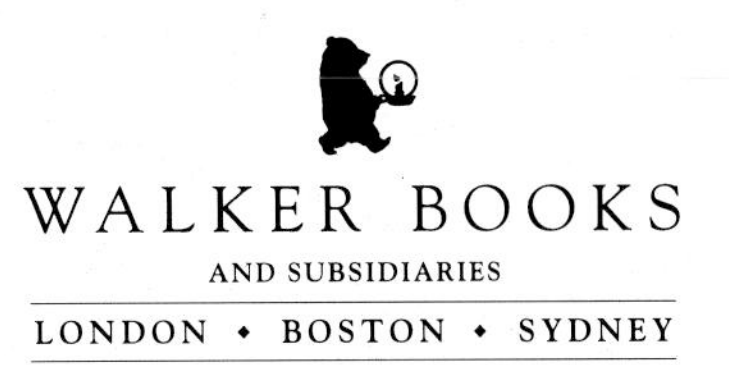

WALKER BOOKS
AND SUBSIDIARIES
LONDON • BOSTON • SYDNEY

Horatio had learnt a disappearing trick.

"One,

two,

three…

hoopla!" he called, and jumped
into his sock.
"Can I do that?" someone asked.

It was Humphrey Thud.
"It's easy," said Horatio. "You just say the magic word and jump into the sock. Let's show James."

James was by his Useful Box,
wondering what to draw.
“Can we show you our magic trick?”
asked Horatio. “Humphrey can
disappear.”

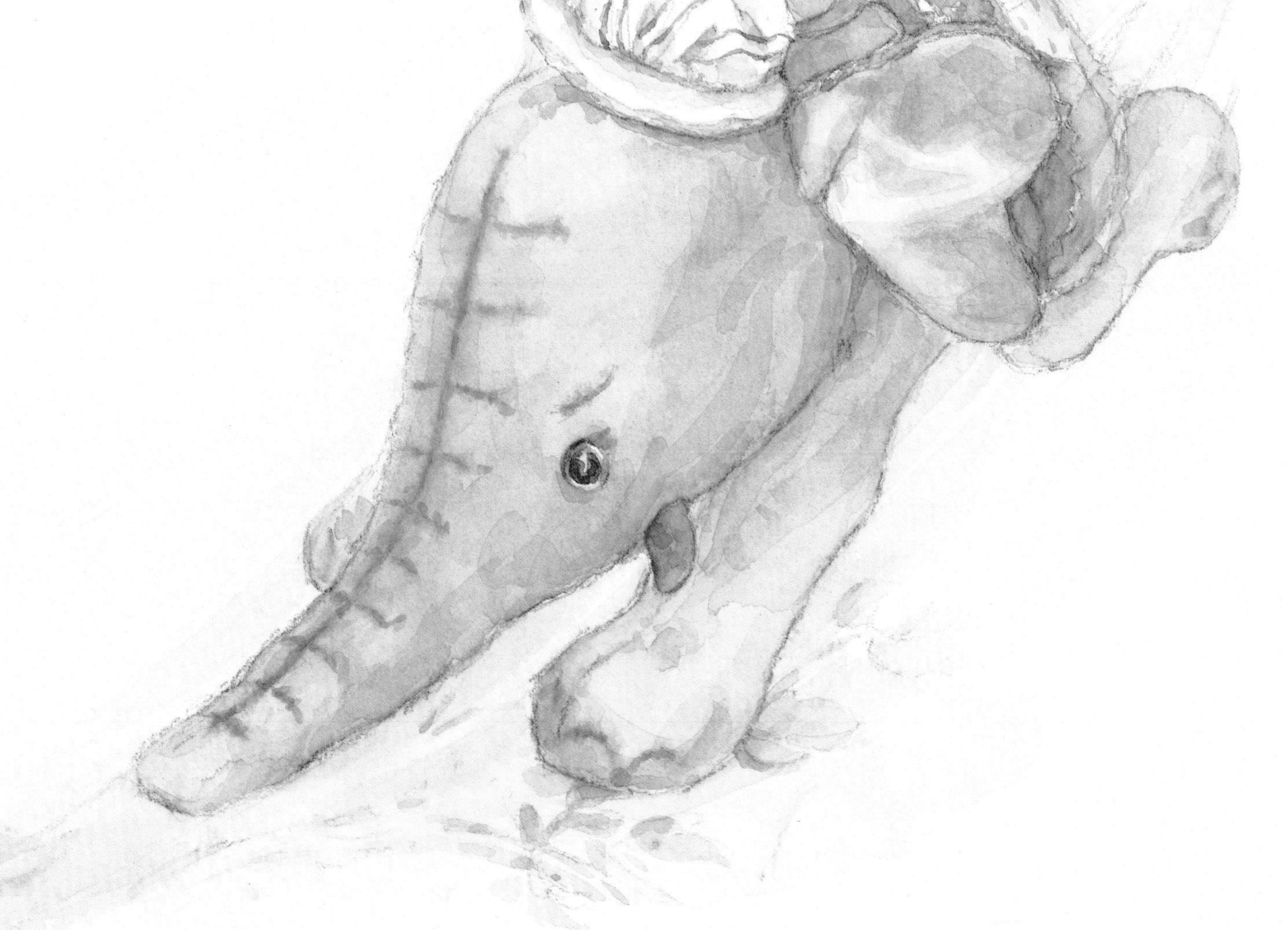

Humphrey charged towards the sock.

“Hoopla!” cried Horatio.

THUD!
“Have I disappeared?” Humphrey asked.
“Some of you has,”
said James.

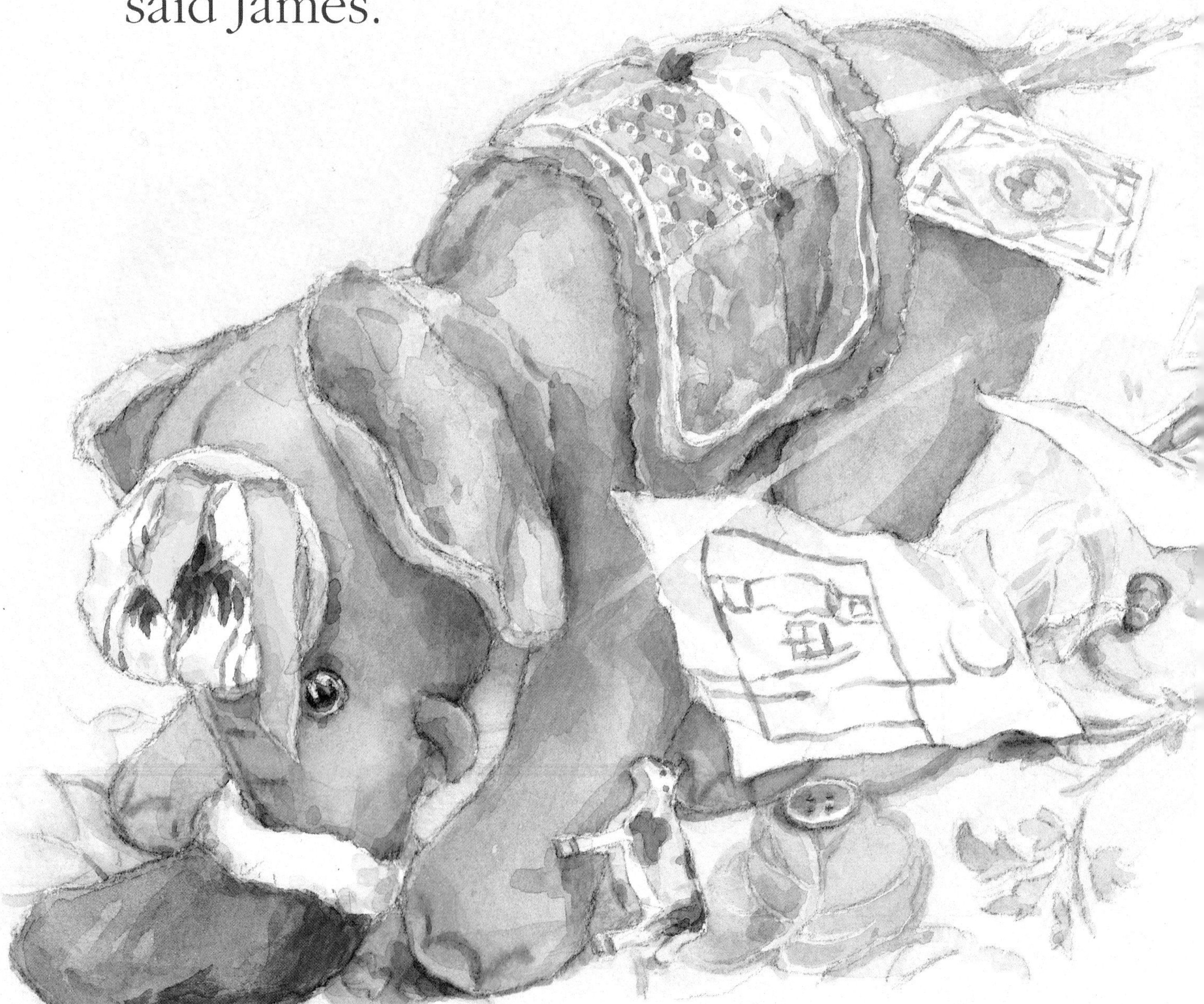

“I must have said the wrong magic word,” said Horatio.
James had an idea. “That sock’s too small for an elephant,” he said. “I have something bigger in my Useful Box.”

James took out a flag and gave it
to Horatio.
"One, two, three … hoopla!"
Horatio called. He threw
the flag over
Humphrey.

A lot of Humphrey didn't disappear.

"Maybe Humphrey's just too big," said James. "Why don't you make his hat disappear instead?"

Humphrey took off his hat and waited, while Horatio looked for a place to hide it.

Horatio was gone some time. Humphrey felt tired.

He sat down.
By mistake he sat on his hat.

When Horatio came back, he
couldn't see the hat anywhere.
"It's disappeared," he cried.

"Hooray!" shouted Humphrey.

James was worried. He hoped the
hat wasn't in his Useful Box.
He opened the lid and looked inside.

James rummaged in his Useful Box.
Humphrey waited.
"This is my best cow," James said.

Humphrey was really missing his hat.

"Can I have my hat back now?"
he asked.

Oh dear, thought Horatio.

Horatio tried to think of a magic word to bring back Humphrey's hat.

"Bee!

Button!

Bumble!

BOO!" he cried.
But Humphrey's hat didn't come back.

"James could lend you something like this," said Horatio. "Maybe."

But James had forgotten all about Humphrey's hat and was sorting out his Useful Bits.

"Humbugs!" he said. "I've found my humbugs."

Humphrey stood up and stretched
his trunk towards James.
"Could I have a humbug?"
he asked. "I like humbugs."

"Humbugs!" cried Horatio. "That's
the magic word. Look, Humphrey's
hat came back!"

Humphrey put on his hat and
took Horatio for a ride.
James sat down to draw.

“Here are my two best friends,” said
James. “Now let’s all have a humbug.”

MORE WALKER PAPERBACKS

For You to Enjoy

Some more James and Horatio books by Camilla Ashforth

HORATIO'S BED

Horatio, the rabbit, has a problem: he can't sleep.
So his friend James, the bear, decides to make him a bed.

"Camilla Ashforth's gentle, object-packed water-colours lovingly suggest an intimate world of mischief and tenderness." *The Times Educational Supplement*

0-7445-3156-X £4.99

MONKEY TRICKS

Shortlisted for the Illustrated Children's Book of the Year Award

The peaceful world of James and Horatio gets a lively jolt, when the naughty monkey Johnny Conqueror appears on the scene!

"Picture book publishing at its best." *The Economist*

0-7445-3168-3 £4.99

CALAMITY

Calamity, the donkey, loves racing. Horatio wants to race too. The problem is that Calamity has a habit of making up the track as she goes along! James, as ever, has a solution.

"The quiet, timeless nursery created by Camilla Ashforth sets the perfect bedtime mood for two to four-year-olds." *The Mail on Sunday*

0-7445-4393-2 £4.99